The Voice of the Turtle

The Voice of the Turtle

and Other Poems

by

Harold Lawrence

This book is printed on acid-free paper which conforms to the American National Standard Z39.48-1984 Permanence of Paper for Printed Library Materials. Paper that conforms to this standard's requirements for pH, alkaline reserve and freedom from groundwood is anticipated to last several hundred years without significant deterioration under normal library use and storage conditions.

ISBN:0-9644858-4-2

Photography by Harold Lawrence

Boyd Publishing Company
PO Box 367
Milledgeville, GA 31061

On these last soft nights
go out among old memories
and take your jar
and be a catcher of the dream
before it fades.

... the joy of days made brief to last forever

TABLE OF CONTENTS

Introduction

Penetrating the local and the concrete has always been the literary strategy for revealing something universal. In this third book of his poems Harold Lawrence continues to probe wide-ranging, concrete, Southern moments that touch universal concerns: past vs. present, nature vs. technology, poverty vs. affluence, and always the astounding variations of the human struggle for meaning and hope. Some of the poems tell the rich humor born of small-town folk: Do not keep a dead cat in a shopping bag ("Shopping Bag Blues"), or carve a deceased husband's gravestone with one's own living name added on ("Precious Memories"). Others describe the chilling realities that faced one's great-grandmother, who could split open a live chick to draw the poison from her own snake-bitten arm — all in a day's work — ("Great Grandmother"), or tell "bedtime tales of barren crops," struggling to give her children a better hope for life than her own ("Hardcash").

Some of Lawrence's harshest and most drastic work describes the lock-hold of life-support technology on small town folk who need to die ("Stairway to Heaven"), a razor killing ("On the Cooling Board"), or the depressed recreation of barroom brawls ("Slab House"). At the same time, he can invoke lost childhood ("Jerusalem Cherries") and the tree-climbing of a youngster who finally comes down from his perch, "half child, half exiled prince" ("Monkey Boy"). Nature is the wonder that surrounds all the human grit and striving, where

> . . . heaven's blue eye is open
> bright blue around the pupil of the sun
> and a gentle peace is on the fields
> as they lie green and cradled
> by trees . . . ("Glory Days")

The many colors of Southern life are what the sun-pupil sees in Lawrence's poems — and sees also the turn toward a new kind of human-made light, the transition to electricity ("REA"):

> . . . a flood of white-washed brilliance
> lit the boundaries of the room
> and made them younger than they were.

The radiating bulbs revealed dirt and grease they hadn't realized were there, and so they

> . . . went from room to lighted room
> and like homage paid to an unknown god
> washed down the walls.

The days when the farming couple took their tiny premature infant daughter and incubated her across the winter in their earthen churn, turned and rocked on its rounded side ("Life in a Churn") are rushing to an end. New techniques promise new wonders and new uncertain gods. Lawrence's poems are born of a culture in transition.

William Mallard
Emory University
September, 1995

Cane Mill

Out on the Gassaway place
where that mule of Billy Boyd's
plods in an eternal circle
pulverizing the dust
to a texture of ground spice
and cutting the path down deeper
until it seeps from under toes
like the powdered earth
of a ceremonial mound
the stalks are fed through
in the plodder's wake
and green juice pours from the eye
of the metal worm
and fills a wooden bucket.

Off to the south a ways
downhill and downwind
it is poured into the sluices
and pushed with wooden paddles
into a sectioned pan
past the keeper of the fire
and the nauseated skimmer
until it cooks to a golden bright
but that old mule of Billy Boyd's
never sees beyond its blinders
and never lifts its head
until it is unhitched for the night
like so many who turn the stiles
and are content to grind along.

At The Mazda

The night James Dean died on the screen
at the late-night picture show
in the popcorn-scented dark of the Mazda
where the local young and restless
lolled in upturned collars and ducktails
sipping fountain drinks and popping gum
a bolt of defiance struck the seats
in the row where they sat bunched
like vegetables going through a heat
and sent them out to smoke
or burn rubber on some lonely road.

Sometime near the stroke of midnight
in the silence that always follows
an anguish of twisted steel
a breathless call was made
from the dark mouth of the ticket window
as the marquis lights still blazed
informing aging sleep-drugged parents
that their boy had just been killed
in a head-on near the river bridge
leaving them with spliced bits and pieces
like the preview of a coming attraction.

Old Red swept out the aisles
his broom fishing for sticky candy wrappers
and his eyes smarting from the smoke
of a hand-rolled cigarette
and the violence of those final scenes
that killed that boy sho' as God

smarting like the eyes of a stricken pair
who stood pajama-clad and helpless
outside the small emergency room
watching as an ambulance backed in
and hands whisked away a sheeted form.

They were about to follow it inside
when car doors slammed and voices spoke
and someone called from far away
urging them to behold their son
bounding across the parking lot
to appear whole and well before them
the victim suddenly no longer theirs
but another by the same first name
just like a scene from a movie
allowing them to breathe and be relieved
that their boy was not the one.

As admonitions started to sink in
and things smoothed out for a time
rebellious youngsters quieted down
as though innocence had returned
while showtime at the Mazda moved
to light and wholesome entertainment
in a drubbing of musicals and comedies
mixed with B-grade cactus westerns
balancing out the wilder side
on safe and solid family fare
of heroes riding off and happy endings.

Just before the year went out
on a night as close as death
with the Mazda wrapped in twisted light
and fog thicker than a human hand

they brought that same film back
and turned its passion loose again
spilling rage and leather out the doors
to revel in a high-speed chase
completed when those easy resting souls
got the second call about their boy
and this time it was him.

The Mazda: The Mazda theater stood on Cox Avenue on the west side of the block between Hwy. 72 and Seneca Street in Calhoun Falls, SC. It was remodeled into a theater from an old mercantile store by William M. Broadwell, Sr. and opened in February, 1940. It closed in 1958 to be reopened by Juanita and Sarah Broadwell in 1959, running shows only Thursday through Saturday. It was closed permanently in 1962-63 and the property sold. The building burned around 1972 and was demolished shortly after. All that remains is a vacant lot.

She did not see the glancing snake
but felt its stabbing bite
from cool leafy blackberry shade
and jerked the fiery red-puffed arm
back out into unforgiving light
spilling what was in the bucket
as she snatched up the paring knife and ran
straight toward the chicken lot
the shattering surprise no longer etched
in her impassive face.

With one deft determined sweep
she grabbed a peeping chick
and sliced through its soft innocence
and pressed the wet and pumping warmth
faint heart exposed and beating
against her swollen wound
drawing out the venom's wrath
bubbling from those puncture marks
until the tiny yellow corpse turned green
and stiffened in her hand.

She scooped up a second and a third
sacrificing half of the new brood
before the red-eyed flogging hen
blood dotting her feed-sack dress
of white with purple button prints
then rose and picked up the scattered fruit
and cleaned up at the well
and then went about her day
for she had a pie to bake
and mouths to feed.

The Way Of Things

Always on the sunny surface
in the blond fluff of their innocence
there will be a fresh new line
of little mallard chicks each spring
with the entire pond before them
glistening and wide.

And always underneath
rising from the shadowed depths
there will come a black murky disk
to fasten upon a paddling foot
and pull them under one by one
never letting go.

On their way to the bottom
just before the life leaves
in the last fury of escaping bubbles
a wild eye meets a cold one
and in that interlocking stare
everything is redefined.

There wasn't much of a crowd
the day they put the drink machine
in the store at Sandy Cross
but when word got out about it
hands would come in from the field
with the last of their pocket change
and reach into the icy dark
like they were grabbling under rocks
pulling at those wet shiny bottles
and wrenching off the metal caps
then given to a moment's wait
for the gray smoke to curl out first
before gulping down the fizz and amber
until the one cool spot
could be touched on their bellies
underneath the overalls.

That long red refrigerated box
humming against the left-hand wall
turned out to be as precious
as the ark of sacred times
not so much for what it held
as for the spot on its sweating surface
that when touched just right
would send a small electric charge
straight through the thirsty customer
cleaving tongue to drier mouth
and causing body hair to stand like quills
and knees to melt into rubber
as the knowledge of this consequence

was seared forever on the mind
like grill marks on a steak
elevating the state of learned behavior.

It got to where more would come
to feel that shock go through them
than to down an ice-cold drink
content to wait their turn in line
out there in the sweltering heat
for a quick jolt from the box
calculating how each day was the same
under a relentless sky of brass
and the eternal monotony of the fields
would only sink their spirits lower
and keep them in a vexing mood
so that they were bound to come
and touch the spot on the machine
to get their weekly treatment
not just an antidote for their depression
but the one sure cure.

The kudzu zoo is always open
if you have a mind to see it
through heavy half-closed eyes
full of tired aging elephants
with emerald dripping from their tusks
mournful giraffes and old lagging bears
and soft familiar monster shapes
all bogged down by the weight of its foliage
like the vine-covered statuary
of a lost bone and feathered civilization
buried in the jungles of the Yucatan.

Still they strain to rear and straighten
from behind the metal guard rail
on a bounding stretch of Georgia highway
bowed and grieving from the lush greenery
as they reach out in phantom pleas
stirring our primitive sympathies
for the times we felt motherless
lying in our bedtime silence
held prisoner by our fears
but comforted by the sculptured shadows
of those sad docile beasts
that nuzzled us through our covers
into a cherished state of belonging.

10

At The Lowcountry Boil

At the lowcountry boil
Junior told it for the truth
since he had been the natural one
to insure the new conversion van
his brother Elroy drove around the block
kicked once and doled out cash
to finalize a honey of a deal
but he turned white as a deveined shrimp
telling about the full coverage
and how he made Elroy take it
doing for a little brother
the same as for himself
and it took a panatela
and a shot of that good white
to pry the longer version loose.

It seems Elroy was coming home
from a late night at the swamp
where he had rolled up on the boys
and let them read the window sticker
out there by the Coleman lantern
and feel the plush and vinyl
and smell the new inside
while trying out a back-seat table
ideal for playing cards
and him gaining more admiration
than the recently divorced
whose lives were once again their own.

About half-way down the Sandtown Road
a buck jumped from a high red bank
sporting a rack like a Christmas tree
and hit dead center on the passenger side
caving in the sliding door
then bouncing backward in a ditch
to twitch and flinch its last
Elroy rocking on his shocks a bit
before stepping out to look at things
and take a lug wrench to the door
where the panel lip was bent
and graduating to a cussing mood.

Not being one for willful waste
he sat down in that roadside ditch
and locked his arm around the deer
and held its nose till it expired
then dragged it to the crinkled van
with characteristic puffs and grunts
then pulled and shoved the thing inside
and slammed the damaged door
and took off down the road
miffed about his lot in life
and fumbling with the cruise control.

He was breaking for the crossroads
four miles south of Julep
headed east toward Hazelwood
when the deer in back revived
head goring out the cushioned seats
and sharp hooves kicking window glass
into a thousand spider webs
with Elroy dodging lethal blows
and getting cut about the head
as he slowed and shifted into park

then scrambled out the door in time
to see that ten point rack
run through the dash and windshield

It took awhile to pry the side door loose
and get the thing to leave
but after it jumped out in the night
and bounded off in the high beams
and Elroy brushed glass off the seat
and broke out enough to see to drive
he brought the van on in
and drove it straight to Junior's
and parked it in his yard
figuring on that full coverage
to handle all the body work
him hitting a deer and all.

The Apple Maker

The first ones were hand-carved
created from a longing in the will
called forth and breathed upon
just as God would form a world
and shaped to perfection in her thoughts
long before she touched the wood
sculpted with dents and dimples
until no two looked alike
then honed and polished bright enough
to stir the urge to taste them
first made to glorify the act
of something brought from nothing
then made to order.

From the random access of an imprint
buried deep in her genetics
like a pattern for her craft
she has revealed her gift
and birthed such patient fruit
only to be forced to fill
the tooth of a ravenous throng
waiting to devour her handiwork
forced to turn them on a lathe
and use electric sanding tools
that make every bruise the same
so pressed that she no longer stops
to name each one.

Mama'en'ems

I got to thinking how it was
when we would put the past aside
and all go over to Mama'en'ems
and sit around the ice cream churn
with healing and forgiving words
as eager as kids at play
around a white washed tractor tire
to tag back in with all the times
we circled one in barefoot mirth
and hugged those dreams ourselves.

Then sister would come from her double-wide
just back of Mama's flower bed
and proceed to tell us once again
that in due course with Mama gone
the house would then be hers
which made the rest fly hot
and quickly take up sides and touch
on numerous unrelated grievances
designed to low-rate and offend
and carry things from bad to worse.

The cream would melt, Mama would cry
and gather up the paper plates
and take her pound cake back inside
leaving us to stare each other down
or count the grass blades underfoot
while sister withered from our looks
and brother beat his whining kids
and was the first to leave
and we swore never to go back
but we always did.

REA

That last night by the kerosene lamp
was like a time of Settin' Up
a hush in every room
like the last breath of a grandmother
and wires strung from the ceiling
with their strange and impotent globes
like something from a doctor's office
or the far side of a dead world.

They huddled close and listened
as the magic was spelled out for them
their faces shining back at them
from the curvature of the lamp
and their futures bright and smiling
in the imaginary checkered hayfields
of the yellow and white oil cloth
dreamt briefly at the kitchen table.

It was nine by the pocket watch
when a flood of white-washed brilliance
lit the boundaries of the room
and made them younger than they were
laughing and squinting at the naked bulb
then finally remembering the lamp
suddenly grown orange and old
like a relic from a crypt.

All eyes raised in awe and adoration
counted grease spots on the ceiling
and webs in the beaded corners
and stains from a thousand fires
so no one went to bed that night
but went from room to lighted room
and like homage paid to an unknown god
washed down the walls.

REA: Stories about the first lights in a rural community are numerous throughout the South. This one was taken primarily from conversations with individuals who remembered the experience as children and from a piece in the *Georgia Review*, Summer, 1993, by Jim Heynen, entitled, "The Boys," which is part of a larger work to be published by Alfred A. Knopf entitled, *The One-Room Schoolhouse: Stories About the Boys.*

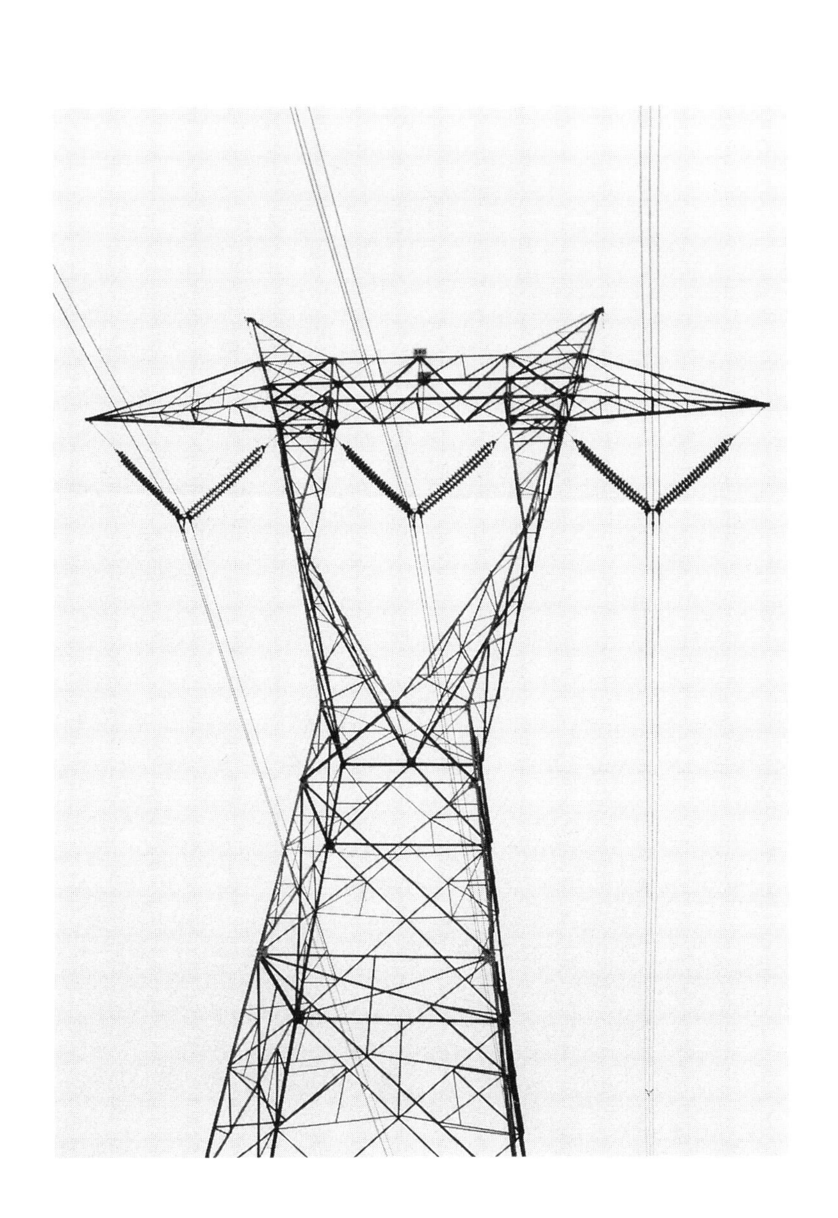

Full Cry

It is a matter of trust between dogs
as to who will be followed
when the trail burns hot
and the scent is fresh and keen
for there are those who specialize
in pulling others from the chase
with high-pitched yelps and feints
that always lead them nowhere
and there are silent trailers
who will keep the aroma to themselves
and deprive the rest of sport
until their prey is denned or treed.

Before going out into the thick of things
it is best if there is one
bred from a good bloodline
with a nose for winding the night air
to disqualify the cold trails
one who will not range the scale
with a yip and a squall
a yodel and a bawl
but who will give a long clear call
that shatters the bone cold evening
and find the path that all will sniff
and sound out grudgingly on silver notes . . .
great heart! great heart!

A Flying Wallenda

I was right up there with him
the day Karl Wallenda walked the wire
at Tallulah Gorge
straining against the wind velocity
on the weight-tipped balance pole
and calculating with a memory
of near-slips and deft steps
a formula to offset the rush
of hot brain-drenching adrenaline
that tips the inner gyroscope
into wobbling fatal spirals
and plunges art and form and style
down to the floor of an abyss
unacceptable to the conscious mind.

I strained with him
in that long steep climb
from the sagging wind-whipped middle
where the face of death grins most
and lungs labor and shoulders ache
and all feats suddenly become
sinking impossible things
in the slow stiff walk up the cable
gulping in cold white air
and seeing from the periphery
the vast sickening reaches
that plumb the empty space
to the tops of toy-like trees.

In secret I have always been
an unofficial member of the troupe
negotiating on the average day
some dizzy heart-stopping stretch
above the din of confused voices
in the great and widening solitudes
and never losing grip or poise
in each quick and nimble step
but always holding in abeyance
the living fear of looking down
upon a hungry thrill-bent crowd
intent on savoring the shattered pulp
of every walker of the wire.

A Flying Wallenda: In 1970 at the age of 65, Karl Wallenda, high wire performer, walked an 1100 foot cable across the 750-foot-deep Tallulah Gorge in Georgia. On 3-22-1978, while walking between two hotels in San Juan, Puerto Rico, he fell 120 feet and was killed. He and his family thrilled audiences since the 1920's, though three were killed and one paralyzed in the course of the troupe's history. See: Jamieson & Davidson, *Colorful World of the Circus.* Octopus Books Ltd., London. 1980, p. 68; Jack Wiley, *Basic Circus Skills.* Stackpole Bks. Harrisburg, PA. 1974, p. 75.

Glory Days

These are glory days
when heaven's blue eye is open
bright blue around the pupil of the sun
and a gentle peace is on the fields
as they lie green and cradled
by trees in their faint first turnings
toward a ripening fall.

Every voice is low and muted
on this widening tide of silence
as birds soar to bounding heights
then hang in acts of grace
and yellow apples bend the bough
like still life in a painting
in these precious weightless moments
when life seems poised to accept each metaphor
as a cherished piece of its time.

To breathe the freshness of each morning
or stand in the bend of rivers
on late red-wing afternoons
when all is sky and glass
or lie down to dappled sleep
in the waiting arms of shade
is to know the joy of days
made brief to last forever.

Precious Memories

A week after the funeral
Myrtice called up White Star Monuments
to ask the price of a double rock
for her husband Lon fresh-buried
with his name and dates at one end
and her name at the other
figuring on how it might be soon
that she would go to meet him
over on that other shore
and how it might be a double savings
if she could speak with Dill
him and Lon both being in the Shrine
and having married first cousins once removed.

Dill dialed her back when he got in
with hot refills from the Dixie Cup
that cooled down quickly when he learned
she had been frustrating by the phone
for a full thirty minutes
waiting to get this straightened out
him low-toned and apologetic
it being a widow's grief and all
and then getting toward a modest price
that both of them could live with
which included Precious Memories free
carved in the middle at a slant
to finalize the sale.

At least two times a week
she called to be assured that he
would not forget this binding sentiment
this touch, this great outpouring
this heart-felt token of her choice
on that enduring granite slab
and he would calm her down each time
with those low tones of his
reciting a litany of former sales
and patrons highly satisfied
until it was almost hallowed
then ending with the pledge
that he would not forget to add
those Precious Memories.

It took a month to get it cut
and strapped down on a pallet
there at the pit near Elberton
but the day Dill picked it up
and drove those two hours back home
and lowered it down to the soft gravel
minus a beam and chain-fall
but with four sweaty helpers at the corners
while he grunted with a pry bar
he called her before the sack-crete dried
to tell her it was squared and situated
just as he had drawn it on the sketch
saying, "No ma'am" when she interrupted twice
to ask if he had not forgot
the words that seemed to say it all.

He figured she'd be pleased enough
with what he did for her and Lon
to recommend him at a later time
but there were funerals right and left
in the cooler months which followed
that claimed a few she moved among
but they chose elsewhere and otherwise
without the slightest hint from her.
He was hard-put to understand it
until she phoned him that next spring
to ask if there would be a charge
for taking her name off Lon's rock
and how soon could it be arranged.

Dill calculated the expense two ways
him bringing in some company to do it
or renting out a blasting tool
as she related how the time had passed
and how she had been seeing someone else
and wasn't sure she'd bury next to Lon.
They settled on the figure that Dill gave
for renting the equipment out
and would he be careful with her flower pots
and would he not cut the thing so deep
that he would leave a hole
and ruin the looks of things for Lon
and if it wasn't too much trouble
could he please take off Precious Memories?

Condolences

One hundred billion galaxies
each with one hundred billion stars
and three hundred million light years across
no more fit into our consciences
than the annual family gatherings
when we crowd into the old houses
and there is no convenient place to sit.

Expanding universes cannot be contained
though minds and hearts do their best
to hold them within mythic bounds
until a larger glass is trained on space
or someone puts an extra fold-out table
in the living room for the grandkids
leaving old fragile worlds forever shattered.

Hardcash

There is a place in Kansas
where the sky is blue
and the grass is green
and the clouds go by like pinwheels
and you can go there
on a road of yellow brick
if you close your eyes.

But I'll tell you of another
with skies of slate
and dirt so hard and poor
a body ached to walk it
and it was spelled the same
at a hundred Georgia crossroads
and its name was Hardcash.

For those who followed mules
with shoes stuck fast in time
and dreams worn down to nothing
it was a place to wait
and listen by the stove
to bedtime tales of barren crops
or tough hard-bitten winters.

For those who stirred the pots
and split knuckles on the washboard
it was a narrow path
from which to bend and carry
untold bucket loads of grief
and bulging sacks of scorn
with eyes too old to cry.

If you were a child in Hardcash
you ate the fuzz and peel
and sucked out the salty marrow
and you learned arithmetic
counting ribs on a milk cow
or fingering metal tobacco tags
kept in a string bag.

Had you been there in the Thirties
standing around in field stubble
minus hope and without credit
staring at a horizon
of broom-sage and scrub cedar
you might have taken steps
to curl right up and end it.

But those who built the fire
and rubbed their eyes each day
and lived on syrup and pone
held fast to what they knew
and knelt by the bed at night
and prayed that you
would never have to go there.

On The Fall Line

The snakes that crawl here every April
up from the dead gray sand
and the soft crumble of strata
(where the ocean used to be)
to sun themselves in the road
no longer have to watch for Ralph.
He won't be driving over them
or grinding them under his wheels
skidding and crisscrossing his tires
to mash life from their beaded skins
leaving them to writhe on the pavement
or be carried off by hawks.

Ralph got a big one last year
a fat dusky timber rattler
that slid onto the tar and gravel
right in front of his company pickup
at the turnoff to the chalk mine.
He lined it up with the right tire
and crushed its head on the first pass
then backed up to sit and watch
as it bucked and coiled into a knot
regretting that he had no sack
to hold its quivering girth until
he could show it to the boys.

He noticed the slow leak in May
and took the truck to Linwood's
and popped the lugs himself
rolling that same bone-crushing tire
out back to Linwood's tank
after swelling it to sixty pounds
but could find no escaping bubbles
though he snagged a calloused thumb
on what he thought was radial wire
and died before the week was out
his mind racing with explanations
but none faster than the rattler's strike.

Ski King

When the lake was new and brimming
with its waters red as blood
we'd watch him churn them
crisscrossing behind that low black boat
and popping the nylon rope
like a long wet yellow whip
as he shot past on each lap
showing us how it was
one hand, one ski, so-o-o easy
and thrilling friends and relatives
he brought with him from McCormick
who stood ankle-deep in wonder
on the little make-shift beach
and shouted, "Go, Ski King!"

The afternoon bore down on him
streamed down and smiled upon him
through green plastic lens-tinted shade
and sheared off jet-black skin
and jinked off pink florescent trunks
as he bounced on the boat's wake
and rode waves of his own making
one hand aloft and hailing
those lesser rooted beings
seen through the wind-whipped spray
and glimpsed in the liquid shining
whose loud voices froze in awe
then rose on every swell
with, "Go, Ski King!"

The whites who came there to picnic
abandoned their fried chicken plates
to the constancy of blue-bottle and deer fly

and sat there wide-eyed and open-mouthed
wreathed by the yellow jackets
and mesmerized by his flawless exhibition
which shattered their most cherished myth
of a pulp wood driver stuck in first
who did not have the sense it took
to shift the stick to second gear
just as the outboard whipped sideways
and shot him toward the bank
like a rock loosed from a sling.
"Come on in, Ski King!

Hands locked behind his head
and waxed skis skimming like eels
surfing on a liquid mirror
he misjudged those final yards
closing like a late-bound freight
and over-shot the thin strip of sand
to soar airborne into the pines
and crash down bruised and broken
the curious and idolatrous hovering over him
until someone fetched from Lincolnton
a white hearse with a red light
that doubled for an ambulance
and spirited him through the line
of waving handkerchiefs. "Go, Ski King!"

Ski King: The above incident was witnessed in the early 1950's in the area that is now Elijah Clark State Park on the Georgia side of the Savannah River following the completion of Clark Hill Dam. Historically, Elijah Clark, for whom the lake and the dam are named, is spelled, "Clarke."

Life In A Churn

At birth she fit into his palm
like a land terrapin on its back
moving all four limbs at once
"no bigger than a mite," he said
as he took a silver dollar
from a string bag in his bib
and lowered it close enough
to cover up her face
then measured both her tiny feet
against his larger thumb.
Once these amusements spent themselves
the fearful thought of losing her
shouted louder in their ears
than the little cries they heard
while squinting by the lantern light
to better estimate her size
shouted out with ringing words
for them to think, to improvise.

They took her pound of flesh
and fit it in their earthen churn
turned over on its rounded side
with glazed ceramic bottom near the fire
and slowly rocked her back
to fleece-lined safety in a womb
made lovingly from what they had
consigning her to thick heated darkness
away from sight and touch and smile

like giving someone up in death
to the isolation of a crypt.
By the twilight vagaries of curved light
she slept and grew in half eclipse
belonging to those faint sour odors
until a balmy day in spring
when she emerged full weight
pink-tipped and worth the sacrifice
of days and nights and butter.

Life In A Churn: Flora Mae Huff, b. 10-18-1890, was a premature child belonging to parents, William Henry Huff (4-27-1866 - 1949) and Eugenia Jamison (8-25-1872 - 10-24-1947). She was their first child, and both were anxious about losing her. Premature babies on rural farms in South Carolina in this time period simply did not survive. These young people placed their baby in a homemade incubator made from a churn. At night, they placed her in a shoebox and put her between them for warmth. In 1977, at the age of 87, Mrs. Flora Mae Huff Spencer told this tale about her early life.

Some lakes have a lot to hide
but when they lowered the gates on this one
to do repair work at the dam
and the top of that '88 Grand Prix
broke the surface like a softshell
off the boatramp at Jets landing . . .
for the second time in memory
she grudgingly gave up her dead.

There is no telling how many boats
have eased across its dark shadow
or how many hooks have snagged it
while dragging on the bottom
but in the larger scheme of things
such revelations yield for everyone
some of the missing psychic pieces
and fit them neatly into place.

It is not enough to view her
at sunset from a county bridge
beckoning like those picture post cards
or use her layered depths
to fish for bass or bream.
This thieving side of who she is
will find a way to sate itself
and no one will break her from it.

Secession Lake: On October 11, 1994, a submerged vehicle was spotted near a boatramp on Lake Secession in Abbeville Co., SC, when the lake was lowered for repairs. The car and driver had been missing since December 1, 1990. About ten years earlier, another person was discovered in the same manner. See: *The Press and Banner, and Abbeville Medium,* 10-12-1994, front page article.

Rabbit Well

As children in these towns
where the world ended at the city limits sign
and everything beyond was blank space
the Sunday rides would sometimes take us
far into the vast seclusions of deserted lands
where leaned old empty antebellum halls
with their sagging fronts and dead gray cedars
yawning from the paved edge of places
near the rim of all known things.

In our small hearts and heads
it spelled anathema to go there
and listen to names forever being called
of the old ones who had died
and of fox at play in their yards
and we imagined also on their graves
in a distant clump of tangled trees
as we glimpsed our own abandonment
transposed upon the car window.

Then we would come to the Rabbit Well
and taste its essence in our mouths
feeling hospitality as well as grief
go down and pool like mercury
as we drank and took back something
to remind us later in the twilight
of all things narrow and familiar
that there abide in desolation
shy silent bids for closed communion.

Rabbit Well: This well stands on the north side of Hwy. 72 near the Middleton community in Elbert Co., GA, a few miles east of Elberton. For many years, it has served as a place of refreshment for travelers who may stop for a drink before continuing on. No one in the community remembers when it was dug or by whom.

RABBIT WELL

Jerusalem Cherries

We were cautioned not to eat their fruit
though their white star blooms
and perfect spheres of Chinese red
took root in our affections
as we played there on the porch
raking through the button box
for a broken rhinestone brooch
to use as pirate treasure
eager to complete who we were
in our bright silk kerchiefs
and felt eye patches tied with string
and dime store rubber daggers.

We rolled their berries there
on idle summer evenings
under the swinging naked bulb
as grown-ups creaked in their chairs
and ground through tiresome conversations
aiming them at the weathered bucks
in the gray pine decking
and then thumping them once
catapulting them out into the dark
where every purpose ended
feasting on our innocence and guilt
as we sniffed our stained fingers.

Though crushed by falls and tumbles
and trampled for a decade
by boys who chased the ball
they brought themselves to bear
the quiet births and deaths
of our goings and comings
down to the last occasional visits
winter in and summer out
like old relatives who watched us grow
and craved our recognition
even as our world enlarged
and they diminished in our eyes.

Grass Widow

He walked above the grass
while she sat for hours
staring at the wallpaper
divorced from soap and dishes
with no one left to fix for
carrying her indignities
as she would a stone bruise
and her heart-sick grief
like a freshly dressed wound.

At night she slept alone
curved toward the empty middle
of the dark mahogany four-poster
waking to each faint noise
like a captive under guard
who strains against the ropes
small in her bed-soaked fear
under the gleaming scimitar
of a watchful moon.

After several lame attempts
to bear back to the world
what time could never heal
she chafed against the smirks

the sad but knowing looks
and very quickly learned her place
among the failed and fallen
judged to be fair game by some
and leprous by others.

The dictates of necessity
brought its seasons of seclusion
in the hum of the sewing plant
with her standing at the machine
like a soul in quarantine
late afternoons of overtime
and nights with take-home work
giving their subtle pleas
that she be left alone.

She went back each evening
to the ever silent house
under the same night sky
to finish a piece of hand work
and wait for sleep to take her
in its long flowing mane
to those far reaches in herself
beyond the shades and shadows
where the magic never changes.

April One

When having fun was a simple thing
an owl was shot out of a roost
that final night in March
its semblance held in escrow
to play the vital part
in the inauguration of new fools
as it was wrapped and tied with string
and transported at first light
to the nearest neighbor's door
and passed off as fresh meat.

As it was customary to share
a mess of newly-butchered pork
with others up and down the road
the neighbor gladly took the gift
and recollected how he'd heard
pigs squealing on the afternoon before
which caused him to acquire a taste
his family rousting as he spoke
to start the fire and heat the pan
and hold feast with their breakfast.

Some time later on that morn
a wiser man went out his door
to meet the train where it would slow
in time to hand a parcel up
to a lone brakeman leaning out
and tell him it was turnip greens
then go home highly satisfied
that he could take the simple ruse
that got the best of him
and send it further down the line.

April One: This story is told by Russell Slaton of Washington, GA, who told of the events of 3-31-1931 when he and his father, Andy, Joe & Bennie Whitener brought home an owl and delivered it the next day to a neighbor, Tom Rousey. Rousey later took it to the railroad near Norman and gave it to brakeman, Bob Dyer, as the train continued toward Elberton.

It looked like any other place
until he put the truck in park
and walked in from the road
and found the painted corner trees
on the back side by the creek
that ran through reed cane patches
and by occasional oversized beeches
jutting from a stand of sourwood
its sandbars tracked and muddied
with the prints of cow and deer.
From that time till the next
it took familiar size and shape
as he recounted the once open fields
with their endless red places
now crowded with persimmon sprouts
and long overdue for bushhogging
and memorized each solitary stretch
of silent birdless woods
until there came a great belonging
held fast in the mind's eye
by the urge to make it his.

The spot he picked for the stand
faced off the ridge above the creek
where thumb-sized acorns pelted
like rain on the rusting leaves
and squirrels delved and rustled
forever scratching out clean places
and the lack of underbrush
would give an open shot
like a window through the trees
to a rub of horn-hooked cedar.

After the sound of hammer and saw
shouted through the hardwood hollows
and then receded out of hearing
he sat down on it and surveyed
each branch and clump of brush
each shadow in a lane of fire
knowing where the game trail crossed
and its relation to a scrape
fresh-pawed and rank with urine
narrowing his sense of place
to a province more particular.

In the veils of opening day
with distant shots reporting back
like wind popping clothes on a line
he fired into a dappled silhouette
then hurried down to the fast fading
of hooves scissoring the leaves
when he fell and fired again
the shot ripping high enough
to shatter his right femur
and start a wet widening circle.
As he lay down pale and narrow
touching the place of wounding
and waiting out the hours
his open eye brought everything to scale
in the veins of a drying leaf
and an acorn's crinkled cap
and other bird's-eye pieces
of a world so frozen and familiar
while a deer stamped close by
winding the air and blowing
unmistakably in the possessive case

He asked it at one of those filling stations
that got left in the overhang shadows
where the new bypass came through
while the four sitting around on boxes
waiting out the last soft days
like old prisoners doing their time
were only too glad to mull it through
and see where they would come out
in this attempt to know what went
with one who might yet be alive
to help complete the family tree
by shedding light on the numerous kin
of his mother's long-lost Uncle Bud.

Sez Jim: I recollect a feller who lived out back
of the Ivy place where the road forks.
Came there after the war.
It would be about right.

Sez Ed: Wasn't he the one with the little girl
who used to come in here wanting candy?
Used to worry Bob to death.

Sez Bob: Naw! That was Price Wilson's child.
Used to run around in dirty step-ins all the time.
You got the wrong one.

Sez Spec: Whatever happened to that little girl?

Sez Bob again: She married the Turner boy.
You remember him. Got a junkyard full of cars
he wrecked. Never did have any sense!

Sez Jim again: I heard he made a preacher.
Somewhere in Florida. Didn't even come back
when his daddy died.

Sez Spec again: What about that big heavy feller
who made brooms? The one that got his fingers
cut off at the mill?

Sez Bob again: Naw! He's been gone.
Went crazy when the highway took his house.
I don't know where he went.

Sez Jim again: I heard they took him to Lake Falls.
Put him in that nursing home.

Sez Ed again: They tell me it's a nice place.
Wife's sister's child works there.
Been there since it opened.

Sez Bob: Getting to be about that time.
You ought to look into it, Ed.

Sez Ed: Hell No!

And on it went for quite some time
up this creek to a large post oak
and back down three branches over
from east to west and west to east
until hunger struck and Bob said:
Son, I don't reckon we can help you!
which had long since been determined
so he folded up his mental tent
and thanked them one last time
then took his question down the road
to the vine-ripe tomato stand
and asked it one more time.

Creeping Jesus

Taking those long crane-like steps
and holding each leg high
before putting it firmly down
he measured off the barren miles to town
as if stepping over graves
negotiating like an invalid
as he made the way more righteous
for those who watched him walk it.

If there was a road for saints
or drunks sleeping it off on the river
it was the one from Mt. Carmel
that hissed its way to Calhoun Falls
in the hot-tar summer sizzle
exacting prices from its patrons
tantamount to those so dearly paid
by Pharaoh's restless children
on their long moth-dry trek.

It was for him a sacred stair
made salutary with each mimic climb
through the white noon fire of August
purifying every simplicity of heart
by sweating in its oven heat
and memorizing the hair-line characteristics
etched in those miles of asphalt
like a scroll of his forefathers
that hallows every name.

These who are lowly and unknown
as they pass us going to and from
on the boundaries of our attention
will always stop us and be held askance
in our polite arthritic stares
long enough for us to sense
some rich dark secret hoard
lying underneath life's lesser meanings
forever waiting to be mined.

Creeping Jesus: Grady Jones was a Negro who lived on the Ben Manning place near Calhoun Falls, SC. He had a brother, Sam, who lived in Mt. Carmel and worked as a mechanic and another brother, Charlie, who was a one-time cook at the Oregon Hotel in Greenwood. In later years, in his 80's, Grady left SC and went to New York and died there. There is not much else known about him. When he was able, he cut pulpwood. He was often seen sitting in the doorway of his home across from the Manning home reading his Bible. He was seen by everyone in the 40's and 50's walking from the Manning place to Mt. Carmel. Because of his slow and peculiar gait, he was called Creeping Jesus. He probably had the medical condition *tabes dorsalis* which is a degenerative process of the nervous system.

Last Laugh

Alone and aching in quiet hospital dark
his stomach stapled with a wire mesh
like those old seines and fishbaskets
noise from the hall shook him awake
and pain engraved across his memory
the great wherefores of his present state
as he recalled how there was no drill
among the junked and jumbled tools
with which to make a solitary hole
to run his neighbor's hot water line
and he had stood behind a wall
directing how it might be done with ease
by someone aiming from the other side
a single shot, bolt-action .22 rifle
which cut the pencil mark dead center
but went on to make a ragged trail
of nine perforations in his abdomen
just one hour past a heavy dinner.

Groaning agony in each pant of breath
each flinch like an ice pick stab
he could not know the noise he heard
in strains of muffled sobs and screams
foretold the death across the hall
of one who ended two long weeks
by turning blue and laboring hard
gurgling death through her breathing tube
and whose teenage night shift sitter
had never watched a life expire
and had bolted from her bedside chair
to a well-lit spot near his door
jumping up and down in little fits

while he listened through a red curtain
of swollen seeping gut-shot pain
curiosity near to bursting in his breast
as he fought the sleep-inducing drugs
hell-bent on knowing what it was.

Eyes blinking back the stinging sweat
and teeth clenched too tight to yell
he inched to the side in increments
each sending those steel-pinched penetrations
like driven nails into the quick
and teetered briefly on the bed's edge
before hitting the floor like a melon
ripe to the point of rupture
and back-stroking across cool dark tiles
with the slow wilt of a salted snail
until he reached the fractured door
and grabbed one of those jumping legs
which jerked itself loose and left
a trail of urine down the hall
as he smiled through the rich gathering black
like light through a keyhole
and slipped out with the painless thought
that his kind always rises to the occasion.

The Voice of the Turtle

I.

Above hard blaring city streets
high on a ledge of glass and steel
where morning sun warms tinted panes
a dove has made her nest
without the memory of trees.
Sometimes in the night she sways
bending with an imagined breeze
and shifting to remain on center
as if her bones remember.
Sometimes she calls out to herself
pitched against the heat and air
humming in the dead gray walls
but her songs are snatched away
and dashed against the mute stones.

An inch away inside the glass
trapped in artificial air and light
a man has pressed his face
against the cool of the window
forsaking telephone and television.
Sometimes he leaves his bed at night
and cuts off the throbbing unit
then sits there by the sill
to listen to her cooing.
Sometimes he talks to her
and wishes he could feed her bread
but there is no latch or handle
no going out or going back
from this cage within a cage.

II.

She will fly with the morning
to poise on wires and power lines
until smudged rosy streaks enlarge
upon the sidewalks and the curbs
then she will drop among the pigeons
blue and buff and bullying
to compete for scraps and peelings
and the salty popcorn droppings
that blow into the grates.
She has been pushed and crowded
in a flurry of wings and feet
and forced to drink from oily spots
to peck the cracks and crevices
like a sparrow searching filth.

There is no wonder that she cries
her name against the buildings
or mourns her own reflection
in the little storefront mirrors.
She has been reduced to fly and light
a hundred times a day
beneath a narrow tightening sky
dodging random taxi grills
and the hurried steps of shoes
until there is no heart for song
no longing for a mate
no ease or simple grace
to bear her high above it all
to stretches blue and silent.

III.

If there is to be a spring
which drips temptation in her marrow
and grants a nauseous rebirth
of old notes rising in her throat
she must leave these graveled rooftops
and these dark shrouded alleys
with their strays and fish bones
and check its signs in crannies
where fumbling insects wake and drop
and on crowded breezy corners
where girls wave from open sunroofs
and old women peddle their bouquets
and in the late-night stillness
where she endures a telltale stirring
of mites in movement on her breast.

If she will fly far enough
on these days of longer light
to an old red wall of brick
crumbling from the harsh abuse
of too many rains and winters
and if she will visit its ruins
and rest upon its plaster crown
before it meets the wrecking ball
and gives way to boom and crane
bending her neck to its south side
and widening one red eye
she may spy the long green creeper
that has shot from a cleft in the mortar
and perhaps then she will sing.

(Song of Solomon 2:11-12)

White Gold

Once despised as worthless clay
and cursed as the scourge of barren fields
in a day when the making of crops
and the roar of tractors after dark
were signs of a prosperous showing
it has found a bride's way to be taken
and coveted in human hearts
long after the cotton and corn
have been eulogized and harrowed under
and the green oceans of soybeans
have dried into islands and lakes of pine
and it has shared its secrets sparingly
its mysteries few at a time
like a lover who still tempts and fascinates
despite the ravaging of years.

From the sinking of the first bore
its dust has settled on impoverished farms
like the dreaded touch of Midas
casting the fortunes of the humble poor
into frenzies of greed and litigation
and its slick film has caked and crusted
on sweaty backs that mine its chalk
in countless high white piles
like the drill of ants

and there is no fold it cannot find
or crevice that it will not fill
as it is breathed and tasted
as it is savored and regretted
by those lost in its swirling cloud
who can never go back.

White Gold: Kaolin is a seventy million year old residue of crystalline rocks such as mica and feldspar which has been mined since the 1930's in an area of middle or central Georgia defined as the Tuscaloosa Fall Line. It was first used in the making of pottery and china, though it is now used in coated paper products, pharmaceuticals and plastics and has brought wealth to the owners of the land on which its mines now operate. It has become the major economy of areas previously impoverished.

On Dowdell Knob

On Dowdell Knob when the wind blows
there are echoes far and faint
of old laughter heard in snatches
hitching a ride back on the gusts.
It has always found its way
like a returning bird
but it is missed each time
by the senseless in their haste
to see the view and read the sign
and take their pictures by the pit.

The few who have chanced to hear it
while breathing in the solitude
and savoring those old picnics
have kept such knowledge to themselves
for there are things better left alone
when glimpsed through the soul's window
or filled up like that pit
so that no one will disgrace them
or in search of a souvenir
remove them stone by stone.

On Dowdell Knob: Dowdell Knob is a vantage point on the side of Pine Mountain in the eastern half of the F.D. Roosevelt State Park off GA Hwy. 190. This was Roosevelt's favorite overlook where he hosted many picnics during the 41 trips he made to the area from 1924-1945. A barbecue pit built for Roosevelt's enjoyment is the only historic feature on this location. After his death, the park service filled it with cement to preserve it.

Christmas At The Monument

Christmas at the monument
will not be the same this year
as old lines have been redrawn
and ranks have closed and locked
against the scions of a Council
who birthed a heresy of twenty years
and used its gleaming granite spire
to anchor wire and scaffolding
for the city Christmas tree
and hide from view the memory
of martyrs to the Southern cause
in this holiest of seasons.

These official desecrations ended
on a night three Christmases ago
with a bottle rocket launched
into the decorated laps of evergreen
twisting on its incandescent journey
to put every symbol to the torch
like an avenger of the common good
and purge them from public trust
with heat enough to melt the wires
and shear off huge baked slabs
of precious granite carving
leaving another legacy of scars.

For safety's sake the Council chose
to circumcise the blackened spire
while its United Daughters vowed
and vied for leverage enough

to force its full repair
guaranteeing little peace on earth
and Christmas at the monument
has been taken twenty feet south
of its marked and battered base
where a new tree streaming light
has left its remnant separate
but a little less than equal.

Christmas At The Monument: Since presenting the Confederate Monument to the city of Abbeville, SC, in 1906, members of the UDC have protested the use of the monument as a prop for the annual city Christmas Tree. This use prompted them to enter a suit against the city in 1974 and great discussion made more inflammatory by the pen of the late Grace Hemphill Rogers. Nevertheless, the custom prevailed until 1991 when a fire caused severe damage to the monument and forced the issue of its repair with public funds. At this writing, the issue remains unresolved. See: *The Press & Banner & Abbeville Medium,* 11-2-1994, p. 3.

The Witness

Just outside of Gainesville
on the bridge at Six Mile Creek
held against the green metal grating
by a constant buffeting of cars
the feather-weight emaciated corpse
of a smothered white leghorn
blown from a passing poultry truck
has lodged in the consciousness
of those who pass in droves
on their way to the good life
pulling their campers and boats
to high-priced lots on Lake Lanier.

Regardless of how high they climb
their up-scale homes, their four-wheel drives
their laptops and cellular phones
it will stink there in plain sight
like ammonia in their noses
and function as their albatross
reminding them of what they are
and what has brought them up
from the red clay and the sawdust floor
as they sit in windsuits on a dock
swapping worthless jokes and sipping drinks
ill at ease in their smug denial.

Shopping Bag Blues

White lady named Mercedes in a hurry
to take new shoes and things right back
before the dress shop closes
backing out of the drive unsatisfied
hits a bump! hits another bump!
gets out to see and bless Jesus
she done run over the cat
(no time, no time)
she pops up that trunk lid
puts that dead cat in a Rich's bag
little gold bell just a-jinglin'
little pink tongue stuck out
slams that trunk lid back
(she'll worry 'bout it later on)
and gets on to the store
pulls in there in the handicapped
flashin' those big turn signals
and pops that trunk lid back
and puts that Rich's bag cat
up high on top of the car
(she'll worry 'bout it later on)
while she snatches up the boxes
like they was precious children
and strikes out for that shop
'fore they shut the world down
and fold hands at five o'clock.

Black lady named Sealey come by
she ain't never been in no hurry
ain't never been no lady, neither
been out back in the dumpsters
while that Rich's bag got left
come by and saw it orphaned
and when she looked both ways
absconded with that bag
and toted it clear over to McDonald's
and got herself a cup of coffee
(took a sip, took another sip)
sat there taking her sweet time
feeling right proud about it
and when she had looked both ways
gazed down between her legs
to see inside that bag
and passed out on the table top
head crackin' and coffee spillin'
and somebody screaming nine one one
still screaming when they come
to thump around and feel around
and clamp on that plastic mask
getting ready to roll her out
when one of them grabbed that bag
and set it on her chest
and ain't even looked

'clare to God!

Cherry Hill

We'd taken it on bicycles
and felt the wind catch our breaths
as we coasted down its black-topped spine
hunched over the handlebars
and faces crab-pinched with fear
like fossils frozen in time
toes rigid on the pedals
for fear the chain would lag
and tangle in the sprocket
hurling us to certain death
at blurring blinding speeds.

And we'd walked it in a brown line
with back-packs on weekend scouting trips
buffeted like litter by passing cars
and seeing from its dusky surface
the dim ribbon of the milky way
the smell of its still-warm tar
rich in our nostrils
curing after a day of heat
and clinging to our shoes like gum
pulling us to its heart.

But the day we climbed the ramp
our fathers fastened to its brow
and waited in our down-hill racers
and box-like cog-wheel wagons
like sweating horses at the gate
for the graphite on our axles
we tasted fear and swallowed
as the spring-bar dropped
and shot us past our years
and narrow shadows.

Cherry Hill: This hill is located in the third block of Seneca Street from its west end beginning in the town of Calhoun Falls, SC. The ramp for the cog-wheel wagon race was positioned in front of the J.E. Haralson home, and the event was sponsored in the 1950's by the Lions' Club.

Slab House

There is little left to show
of those old last chance roadhouses
and neon-lit juke-joints
that dotted one side of the river
like cheap corrosive costume jewelry
tucked in between bridges and boat ramps
and as vital to the common good
as the one-stop bait and tackles
that filled the daylight hours with talk
and ice and milk and bread for those
who drank away the evenings
nursing grudges, beers and smokes
like dying relatives.

It was never safe to say
their likes were gone for good
even as the regulars died off
and everything played out
and the worst ones with windows boarded
stuck out like eyesores
as they went to wrack and ruin.
Just as things grew calm and civilized
one was raised up in modern times
from slabs and chicken wire
there on the fringe of Calhoun Falls
and it would be the Evening Star
until it burned.

Packed full on weekend nights
it pulled in old and young
resurrecting from a shrouded past

the bad blood, hard times, jilts and scrapes
which fizzed with each new round
and beaded on the amber bottles
and sweated off the twelve ounce cans
until it ran out on the floor
and puddled by the snakeskin boots
of one red-rimmed from listening
to that quarter-a-shot country misery
causing him to swear off suds and sentiment
and stagger out.

One half-lit star-bent evening
back when the place was hopping
and that music was tearing out the heart
of every man without a date
who rubbed sweaty elbows at the bar
and the dance floor was thick with haze
a burr got up the backside
of a loud-mouth known as Vern
who shoved up next to Ray so hard
it sent pretzels flying down the bar
and sloshed the jar of pickled eggs
as he got right in his face
and asked if he was ready to ride
the malt-liquor bull.

Ray was never much for words
but ventured forth on this occasion
with a string of new ones
and a favorite about Vern's mother
before he hacked him with a stool
and laid him sprawled and lifeless
cold-cocked and as pale as death

across a lighted stretch of floor
head lolled toward the jukebox
which finished out its tune on cue
then switched to another suffering piece
just as an old four-plied veteran mumbled,
"He ain't breathin'."

A biker by the name of Earl
parked to the side with a diet drink
and two of his hard-case buddies
who fidgeted and jingled like loose change
threw one of the tables aside
and jumped on that lifeless chest
his two-eighty weight sagging over Vern
and joining mouth to mouth
as tables moved and patrons pressed to see
then turned away in visible disgust
as Vern got pawed and groped and kissed
it taking extra time for them
to fathom it was CPR.

Someone told Earl to let him die
and he looked up long enough
to squint through a red mist
veins standing out like knotted rope
and say, "He owes me money!"
gulping on his way back down
and blowing life back into worthlessness
until it finally came around.
As everything eased back into place
they hauled Vern out and walked him
carefully feeling pulse and pockets
before pronouncing him stone broke
without a dime.

There were other fights and incidents
that swelled the place to record crowds
and rescued the average day from boredom
like the time two women shot it out
breaking window-lights and drawing blood
or when those boys jumped the chain-gang
and came in to shoot some pool
or the night a drunk got locked inside
and set off the burglar alarm
and scores of less memorable occasions
all accompanied by that grieving jukebox
sobbing out its metal heart
till closing time.

It was plugged in and pulsating
when most of the good-time stories
got burned up in the fire
and curled out on the smoke
leaving nothing there to stare back
but grass growing on the vacant lot
and a few wild flowers and pop-tops
but sometimes on the weekends
when the streets roll up at night
and the breeze comes off the river
it strums an old guy-wire
and recites a few lost bars
from jaded memory.

The Return

There is a strength in the dead grasses
that have lain brown all winter
shot through by stinging frosts
until they have dried and rustled
and blown on the cold biting wind
like pathetic writhing skeletons
that dance in endless cadence
to the cruelest of its tunes.

It will gather from the roots
and rise like a sleeping army
that has mustered in the night
and end this long humiliation
springing up and closing ranks
with green blades sharp and thickening
until it overwhelms its foes
and takes back every inch of ground.

Laughing Box

The last one rotted down and fell
from its fragile tilting pole
a few years shy of World War I
and lay there like a carcass left too long
on glaring main street asphalt
whose remnants had to be carried off
to the edge of public sight and mind
and blacks were glad to see it go
into the teeth of a well-deserved oblivion
but there were a few who could recall
times when it served their purposes
and brought them subtle vindications
that whites were slow to fathom
if they ever did.

Like the day born just for them
when Lucas Binns was on the square
cursing those two deaf mules
he took away from his share-cropper
to equal out a debt
him screaming like something wild
as they stood like sticks of wood
inattentive to his growing humiliation
and every black in hearing

lined up with a blank expression
waiting a turn in modest piety
to stick his head in the box
and cut loose like Brer Rabbit
when he found his laughing place.

And that preacher Jarue used it
when he cut up a worn-out suit of clothes
and sold it for healing squares
staying so long he was pulled out
so a boy named Primus could laugh
at what he did the night before
down at the Gospel Light House
when a white-gloved old sustah
reached into her purse for change
and pulled out a fresh pig's tail
but these and other sly conceits
were things beyond the small design
of that tightly governed street
although they entertained and edified.

Laughing Box: In some Southern towns in the late 19th Century, these boxes were placed on poles on the town square or main street. It was illegal for Negroes to talk loud or conduct themselves in a manner whites considered unbecoming. If a Negro had to laugh while he was on the street, he was to stick his head in the laughing box and do it. That way, he could express himself without creating a public scene. One of these boxes is remembered to have been in the town of Fort Valley, GA.

Stairway To Heaven

The Four West nurses look the same
to those brought up from other floors
as they are shoved down dim-lit halls
where every other ceiling light is out
to that final green-walled room
devoid of art and mirrorless
and minus tv, shower and tub
because there is no need.

They bend down stark-white over them
into the myopic squares of blurred space
like huge attending angels without smiles
who rearrange the knotted feeding tubes
and move the fleece-lined elbow pads
and check the catheters and bags
with the impassive touch of latex
required at the top of the sacred stair.

Who shall ascend to this holy hill
and who shall dwell in this high place?
Those whose only attribute is age
and a silent hatred of their flesh!
Those whose only prayerful hope
is the failure of a life-support machine
or a wet but merciful mistake
injected into the iv port
that grants that last long glistening good night!

Some say they circled back
and buzzed the place too low
because of girls waving to them
like sirens from the bank
tempting them to turn and swerve
the way a flat stone skips a lake
but whatever caused the plane to stall
and skid past a world at war
on its way to full encapsulation
in a trough of watery dark
like a weapon in the Cosmoline
made no provision for the crew
that kept them safe from violation
by the petty thievery of time
or the incremental slights of life
that shrink things down to nothing.

They scrambled out red-faced and young
stepping off its floating wings
as it rocked gently on the swells
churned by the blurred propellers
which hit and bent blades backward
sucking water through the engines
and left to book other flights
while it slid off the duty roster
its charts and maps and instruments
no longer needed for the ride
as smooth as Betty Grable's legs
to the soft mud-lined bottom
and dug in like a hibernating turtle
letting out air bubbles from its turrets
that momentarily marked the spot
where it would settle in and sleep.

Long after everyone came home
and those white-framed clapboard houses
punctuated endless roads and fields
where Molly and me and baby made three
long after their paint cracked and peeled
and the music changed forever
they raised it from the depths intact
its ideals fresh and glistening
and yanked it with a steel cable
into a world grown tired of itself
bringing its full countenance to bear
upon one of those forgotten boys
somehow grown gray and vague
and dwarfed before its frame
too far removed from how things were
for it to claim him.

Lost Boys: On June 6, 1944, a B-25 bomber dubbed "Skunkie," crash-landed in Lake Greenwood near the Buzzards Roost hydro plant and the Panorama Lodge restaurant on SC Hwy. 34. While the crew escaped, the plane sank into the lake and remained there until its resurrection in August of 1983 by a diving and salvaging unit of the U.S. Naval Reserves. Speculation about the cause of the crash and subsequent military investigation as well as the plane's restoration can be found in the following news clippings: *The Greenville News & Piedmont*, 3-20-1983; The Greenwood *Index-Journal*, 8-3-1983; 8-6-1983; 9-1-1989. One of the five crewmen, Daniel Rossman, of Atlanta, GA, made two trips to see the recovered plane.

Poison Berry

What got into Mary Claire
to grudge her brothers so
that she would go to callous lengths
to end their childish clinging
and be rid of them for good
draining the color from their cheeks
each time she gave them candy
then waiting as a spider does
for her sting to do its work?

And what possessed them at the trial
to incline a sympathetic ear
as she told how much she loved them
and would never do them harm
though the rummaged viscera
of the second little boy
bore traces of her poison
even as she feigned innocence
like a scorpion that hides its tail?

Soon after she was taken home
absolved by law of any crime
she slipped off to the trestle
and found the can of strychnine
still safely hidden on a ledge
then ran back to the house
like a smooth and darting viper
spared the dull blade of a hoe
and set free to kill again.

Poison Berry: Mary Claire Berry (8-25-1908 - 3-5-1933) did try to kill again, attacking her husband, Lester Tidwell, with a butcher knife, gaining her second admittance to Central State Hospital in Milledgeville where she died. She is buried in Memory Hill Cemetery beside the two younger brothers, Dolphus (2-11-1922 - 9-29-1924) and Emory (10-16-1918 - 10-6-1924). Accounts of the murders and the trial can be found in the issues of the *Union Recorder*, 10-8-1924, 1-22-1925, 1-29-1925, 2-12-1925, 2-19-1925, 2-26-1925.

The legal title to the plot
of its eight foot square is tenuous
and time gives sanctity to myth
though no such deed was ever filed
which gave the tree a claim
to the ground beneath its shade
yet this spun tale persisted
until the day it fell.

Not wanting to be unprepared
for its slow but ultimate demise
and loath to let a legend die
the Junior Ladies Garden Club
had saved a sapling from its fruit
to transplant in its place
and perpetuate the lavish sentiment
squandered on this tree.

What is it in our minds and hearts
that grants us times of inner pause
when we desert established norms
and jump the boundaries of thought
to ascribe a life to things
that can never know our sympathies
and wait for earth to move
and stones to speak?

Tree Of Life: A standing oak on Finley Street in Athens, GA, is a descendant of one which was purported to have owned itself, being the beneficiary of W.H. Jackson who supposedly left it a deed to its property. This story first appeared in 1890 and has been embellished over the years, though no such deed ever existed. See: E.M. Coulter, "The Story of the Tree that Owned Itself." *GA Historical Society Quarterly*, v46 (3), pp. 237-249; *Banks County Gazette*, 6-3-1891.

The night someone got laid open
by the gleam of a straight razor
out in front of Club Ebony
where pink and blue neons flashed
the law rolled onto the scene
and tracked him in their headlights
large and slow and ponderous
like an unpredictable Goliath
weaving in the middle of the road.
When they cut the engine switch
and put him in the high beams
things got still as death
and that awful sucking noise of blood
squishing from his shoe tops
sounded like life rushing off somewhere
to mingle in the great lonesome
as the rest of him stretched out.

They placed him on the cooling board
huge and muscular in death
and brought in old one-eyed Thelma
forever wise in the ways
and part owner of the Club
to see if he could be identified.
They pulled the sheet down to his chest
where those long, deep lacerations started
and while her one eye blinked and memorized
she asked to see the trail of scars
that traveled down his swollen length
like a switch yard of city rails
sighing as the sheet was yanked
and standing there a long time
before saying she did not recognize him
but allowing how someone had surely lost
a dear friend.

Monkey Boy

Once out of school and under the foliage
of the green and graceful magnolia
that spreads her skirt by the road
he enters the dank dark mystery
of a place somehow feminine
in its sanctity and silent waiting
and is transformed as he climbs
up through the collusion of limbs
found smooth and deathly cool
from boy to jungle swinger
or raucous tropical bird
or whatever fantasy she permits
by the offering of herself
to his awkward bids for freedom.

He rides her branches at the top
until they rustle and shake loose
most of the high white petals
causing nearby heads to rise and turn
at his catcalls and monkey-shines
and warn him not to fall
as he savors each new ruse
that tests the edges of himself
and dabbles in and out of their concerns
knowing he will come safely down
on her flawless springing steps
and go back to the lower world
half child, half exiled prince.

The Logical Explanation

Since the beginning of matches
who has ordained that
a certain number fill a box?
Why not one match more
or one less?
Why not three more?
Who decides such things?
Who determines the length of the stick
or the diameter of the head
or the size of the box?
Who decrees their uniformity?
Who calls forth the law of friction
in patches on the side
to ignite the sulphur tips
and by what authority?
Who makes these decisions?

The matchbox god.

Rubbernecker

Ever since he was a kid
watching through a fogged-up windshield
as a carload of people burned
on a country railroad crossing
he'd found a penchant for it
which got baptized afresh each year
with every house fire and car wreck
that paved a stretch of boredom
on the front page weekly news.
He saved their clippings in a box
their horrors tattooed on his brain
and whenever there were family drives
where he could squire primeval lusts
these were his favorite places.

He was out street-hawking by twenty-one
cruising parking lots and county roads
wired into a citizen's ban and scanner
like a cable to a fusebox
jerking with each fry of the static
and checking out the accidents with injuries
that full swivel neck of his
always the first to the scene
or else just shy of the blue light.
He'd watch them bag and tag 'em
scrape them up and haul them off
until he was addicted to the thrill
a regular ambulance chasing fool
a walking book on highway holocaust.

What finally broke him from it
was the run he made to Rocky Knob
on a late night with stars far-flung
taking back roads all the way
and honed in on the hype and chatter
crackling about those mile-high arcs
flashing from the power relay station.
He figured on a crazed squirrel
running laps out on the cables
and grounding itself to a hot wire
causing a melt-down in the transformers
or a dead tree across the chain-link
but he quivered at the outside hunch
that maybe a plane went down.

They found him later in a fetal ball
out there in the ionized quiet
eyes squeezed shut and trembling
reciting verses in the unknown tongue.
After checking out his vital signs
and finding all the circuits up and humming
one of the power people drove him home
ghost-white, dead-drip silence all the way
and not a clue as to what he saw
though speculation was a saucer hovered
or that he caught too much juice
but with the truth still locked in tight
and no one to coax him back outside
he has yet to tell us.

Swifts

In the last long stare of dying light
before the buildings stand in silhouette
and cold stars blink themselves awake
a chattering sweeps the stillness overhead
as a thickening cloud of chimney swifts
descend for one last exhibition
like circus acrobats in black tights
poised for their death-defying plunge
into sheer ground-rushing emptiness
reeling and flipping in glits and twinks
skimming and twittering as they drop
to catch hold of the invisible bar
just inside their small dank caverns.

The Eye Of Faith

While out bird thrashing
on their way through bent-back undergrowth
to the deep and heavy-laden canebrakes
that bore the sagging make-shift roosts
of endless flocks of passenger pigeons
heads turned back against their breasts
and fitful in their cooing
a father led by lantern light
glad children with their sacks and sticks
strung out between him and their mother's bulk
which bent and shooed ahead the smallest
and steered their steps aright.

Passing through a dimpled cleft of thickets
dense and shaded in the bobbing light
and holding back the stinging branches
one for another along the line
someone let slip a springing hawthorne
catapulting through the flickering dark
and sent a slender barb of pain
glittering on its bristling spine
straight through the tender flesh of one
of the mother's wide and trusting eyes
like hot coals coiled and spitefully flung
from the arm of the devil.

All night she suffered its great loss
the burning needle still in place
under the pucker of ever-changing towels
and the grieving for it done in silence
until the doctor came by morning train
and removed the blind and burning orb
squinting from the lamps and mirrors
of the kitchen table's unaccustomed brilliance
and inserting into the moist emptiness
one forever cool and glass-smooth
through which she learned to live
by faith and not by sight.

The Eye Of Faith: Julia C. Brooks (9-30-1848 - 11-21-1912) met with this accident at the age of 52 when she was the wife of John W. Meeler (7-13-1848 - 4-10-1926) and the mother of 10 children. Rather than leaving home to go to Atlanta and have the eye removed, she had an eye specialist summoned by telegraph, and he came the next day to their plantation near Woodville, Greene County, GA, to remove the right eye and replace it with a glass one. The passenger pigeon was extinct by 1914. See: John W. Meeler, *Meeler & Related Patronymics*, pp. 42-47.

The Dixie Drive-in closed in eighty-three
when they cleaned out the block house
and stripped the speakers from the posts
and sold it all for junk
though kids would still go out there
to gun their engines and scratch off
or just sit on the hoods and smoke.
Weeds grow in the asphalt now
and the lanes are pocked with holes
but when Deeter ran it in the fifties
watching over each row of cars
from his perch in the projection booth
like that eye on the dollar bill
it was well-lit, innocent and orderly
as wholesome as a night in church
with not so much as a paper cup
rolling in the fresh-raked gravel.

All that changed in the sixties
with beer and dope and fights
and a regular letting down of standards
but what Deeter saw going on in cars
through his daddy's old army field glasses
was enough to let the reels run down
and leave the screen stark white
until the complaining honks and yells
would finally start the next projector.
It got so bad that a local linthead
starched out in a T-shirt and overalls
and buying hot dogs for his wife and kids
walked past a car rocking back and forth
and recognized his sister's child inside
with a boy slobbering all over her
and threw his hot dogs on the ground
and turned into a raging psychopath.

With power exceeding human strength
he reached into that steaming car
and locked onto a head of stringy hair
and pulled it out on the driver's side
as surrounding car doors flashed and banged
and five other little pukes jumped in
much to their swift and sorrowful regret
though all lived to spit up blood and teeth
and have their eyes and lips sewn up.
He whipped nine during the intermission
caving in three of their door panels
and breaking out two side glasses
before he stopped to howl and foam
like a grizzly in a circle of dogs
and put his sister's child across his knee
and beat her bare butt with a sandal
until the law got there and broke it up.

A few more weekend scenes like that
and the whole place went to hell
with state patrolmen and city police
taking shifts and cruising across terraces
with their high-beams ruining each feature
and their flashlights shining in suspicious faces
like they were spotlighting deer at night.
Most of the younger crowd quit coming
or switched over to the Sunset on U.S. 29
and things got so boring in the booth
that Deeter wished he were a kid again
back there on a dirt road stomping May-pops
instead of orchestrating life's slow crawl
from the ticket booth to the concession
for the sake of a good clean show
while something as powerful as lust moved on
which proved you just couldn't kill it.

SUNSET
DRIVE-IN THEATRE

For Keeps

I kept it in the left hand pocket
warm against the upper thigh
and separate from those scratched orbs
clamped together like gritted teeth
and bulging on the right.
It never failed me in the ring
as it was nestled in the pointer's crook
and launched from a thumb-nail groove
to crack among the prize marbles
its warm cloud-white globe
with the blue agate center
spinning like a new planet
among the old nicked block-busters
and the lighter smiling cat's eyes
always spotting me the second shot.

It ended on that fateful day
when one of the older, sharper boys
scratched off a larger ring
with a rusted sixteen-penny nail
and placed in the pitted mix
his large and gleaming green-amber
fresh made at the Fiberglas plant
and when my cherished shooter struck
the nearest polished sphere dead-center
it shattered to the heart
the false extension of my will
the foolish pride of all my doings
so that through blinked-back tears
I reached into the ring-scarred right
and blindly picked a lesser champion.

At The Singing School

Preachers were the first to balk
when their crowds slacked off
and all the able-bodied souls for miles
went to the singing school at Bradley
but when every tone-deaf youngster
unhitched his father's sore-back mule
and slipped off down the road
intent on enduring the lessons
for the glories of a basket lunch
or the shy smile of a girl
farm work would start to suffer
and empty places at the table
would cause fresh doubts to rise
about enamored youth returning home.

One man went for his son
taking along a worn-out razor strap
and humming fa so la, do re me
to keep his rage from boiling
at the thought of unplowed corn
but when he walked down to the front
to pull his boy out by the ear

a wren flew from the wooden stand
of the white-faced singing master
and rose on a shaft of light
to hold his imagination hostage
in a long pause of enchantment
until he was forced to find a place
and sit there like a fool and sing.

The Singing School: In the late 1800's, singing teachers would appear in a given county and in two or three adjacent to it and hold singing schools. After a time in each community, there would be a convention where various groups would compete. Being a backwoods entertainment belonging to a primitive state of society, the schools were never attended just for the singing but also for the festive atmosphere and the intermingling of persons for conversation and fellowship. Young people were especially attracted because it was a departure from their routines. The Methodist Episcopal Church, South, published articles in their 1889 instrument, The *Wesleyan Christian Advocate*, denouncing such practices as an interference with work and worship.

Shortfall

What they did to the sky
was to fill it up with wires
and power poles and towers
until the land was threaded
trussed and bound end to end
a captive below the currents
like Gulliver under Lilliputian ropes.

Then they framed the cities
raising them above the cabled snares
in cubes of gleaming glass
lifting them higher each time
and providing clear and polished places
where birds would break their necks
or bang against the surfaces confused.

Above the peaks of domes and spires
ash from the distant stacks
and the fumes of jet exhausts
fouled the crisp clear reaches
with sickening yellows and browns
like that dull x-ray shadow
on the cusp of a dead tooth.

Those who have waited below
eyes locked onto their screens
go outside for short intervals
to take little breaks and walks
stigmatized and pigeon-toed
staring down at unaccustomed ground
and speaking for their own feet:

... if you let me by this time
I'll let you by next time!

... if you let me by this time
I'll let you by next time!

Old Hat

Entering his store
no more than slightly curious
I eyed his line of hats
with no intents or purposes
just idling the time
yet I could sense in him
a will to show me.

He sized me instantly
using the accumulated skills
of those who taught him how
then eliminated styles and shapes
in scores of oval boxes
until he finally found
the singular elusive one
that made the perfect match
then stood back satisfied.

And I by nature
never a wearer of hats
would always wear this one
out of respect for him
and awe at his quick read
of what was best for me.
"How like God," I mused
and like God
he read my thoughts and said
"I do it all the time!"

Recompense

It was awkward horror for us
to stand aside and watch
as corpses left their graves
that time the tight-lipped Flint
hiked up her brown skirts
and in the act of showing us
the wicked side of who she was
disgraced herself.

Some slipped from their boxes
to snag in trees and fences
and gape back at us
while others rode for miles
shut tight under metal lids
like passengers in steerage
washed from their eternal holes
in her purgative menstruations.

After the flood water subsided
and her witchery quieted down
the dead were gathered up again
pulled back from the far corners
and taken to the fairgrounds
to await a grisly matching up
of shriveled flesh and stench
with names and numbers.

It was too illogical a place
to be of psychic aid to us
as we held a cosmic deja vu
with all our fears
but for the objects of the exercise
like that nameless gray-clad corpse
who never got to go in life
it was some small compensation.

Recompense: From July 2-7, 1994, heavy rains caused the Ocmulgee and Flint rivers to overflow their banks. The Riverside and Oakview cemeteries in Albany both had caskets and bodies leave their graves and float downstream, some caskets shooting as high as 6 feet in the air as they came up. Most of the ones in Oakview were stopped by a grove of trees which kept them from floating away. Recovered remains were taken to the Albany fairgrounds for collection and identification. Statistics differ on the number of graves involved. Seven caskets were recovered from Baker County and eight from Pulaski. Out of 405 recovered caskets, only 97 were unidentified.

Working Without a Net

Too soon we were out there
on the sharp pinnacle of worlds
peering over eaves and rooftops
and loitering like smug seasoned hands
on the corrugated ribs of silos
and craning like those mill town pigeons
from the rails of rusted water tanks
sky-watched and luck-charmed
grasping for what it meant
to tread out on high places
while teaching the younger boys
how to uncross a six inch brush
with a flat-bladed scraper
or the proper way to cut a chalk line
with white and green high gloss
or how to paint behind the top rungs
on a thirty foot extension
without sliding down the wall.

It was the second tar-boiling summer
with ladders shouldered and the blind leading
and tin roofs cooking on the village houses
and red wasps in every gable
when the mercury broke the bubble
on the corner store doorpost
causing the improved water-based white
to dry like chalk in the brush
and knot in putrid chunks
along the bright blistering clapboards

and those of us poised up high
with salt sparkling in every pore
smelling mummified sparrows in the boxing
would sway there in the heat and watch
as the mill women walked outside
in their shorts and pedal-pushers
to get a decent breath
repeating fragments of our creed:

always bend with the sway of the ladder ...
always keep a loaded brush.

Welcome to the Subculture

If you're moving in from some place else
having been wet-nursed all your life
on those warm fantasies of hospitality
that ooze from certain counties on the map
or just hell-bent on relocating here
as a blended weave among the locals
drawn by the same perverse logic
that holds in bewilderment and awe
staunching blood with a scripture verse
and wants to fathom how it's done
you need to know before you light
the places you should never go
which speak the truth of who we are
in tones so ominous and low
it is almost impolite to overhear.

Stay out of dim-lit bars and diners
on the fringe of aging cotton mills
where the makeup on the waitress
hides a black eye two weeks old
and the men sit there and watch you
because you are displaced and different
and they piss through the same quill.
Stay out of projects and trailer parks
unless you go to see a relative
unless you understand discouragement
and the pain of being temporary.
Don't go near construction sites
or fish camps or sale barns
where all who tarry use tobacco
and you have to watch your shoes.

Stay away from used-car lots
and those hot shot feel-good salesmen
who smile at you in sunglasses
concealing the truth about that adage
of the eyes being windows to the soul
for their eyes are endless caverns
and their souls are snake pits.
And never go to tent revivals
where the voice popping the microphone
reverts into a lisp and begs
to take your heart and extra cash
straight to the throne of Ja-sus!
Aside from this there isn't much
to tell you. We're just glad you're here
and look forward to your moving in.